HER COASTAL COTTAGE
Where Truth and Love Rise

A novella by

MICHELE LEE SEFTON

tumbleweed
Spirit press

DEDICATION

This story is dedicated to those who believe
in the transformative power of love, and how
loving another can lead us toward our truest,
highest self. A truth that begins, first and always,
with learning to love oneself.

Michele Lee

PROLOGUE

IN THE FALL OF 2020, eleven months after publishing my first poem on my blog, tumbleweedspirit.com, I wrote a poem, titled "A Writer's Dream." That 2020 poem features a speaker who finds success as a writer—so much success she can purchase a multi-million dollar spread. The speaker steps into a mansion and matching lifestyle. Although her monetary achievements feel untrue, the writer in the poem becomes consumed by the allure and appeal of extravagant living. Designer purchases and life's "finer things" capture her attention and consume her words—for a time, until something in the core of her being shifts. A stirring that had long been buried wakes up. This awakening is best understood by turning to the last lines of the original poem:

From "A Writer's Dream":

Then
on a day that began like every other day
something felt off; something was amiss
it was her—she had lost her way
the halls, the dining, and the heels
had consumed her inner bliss
distractions losing their allure and their appeal

the joy that brought her there was no longer found
on the sprawling and enchanting ground
where roses charmed her with their scent
capturing her words when she released a breath
spiraling down stems into the earth, stories left
unsaid
waking the worms and turning the next bloom into
the most vibrant
she kicked off her heels—
no longer needed where she was going
she snipped a charming dozen
before hitting the road
Then
she traded in her mansion key
for a just-right
writing cottage by the sea

The last two lines of this poem, "… a, just-right / writing cottage by the sea," evolved into three sensual poems written in 2021, each titled "Her Cottage by the Sea." It is from those three poems and this writer's imagination that my first novella was born, now offered as a second edition with added scenes. It is my wish that this story be enjoyed during one carefree sitting, when and where readers can pause the busyness of planning and living and get lost in the rhythm of poetic storytelling.

HER COASTAL COTTAGE

Where Truth and Love Rise

CHAPTER 1

MACKENZIE'S HEART, TOO TIRED to beat to the pulse of vigilance and protection, was exposed to everything swirling inside her—a deep yearning, a restless calling, an aching softness, and a thunderous explosion that, for days, had caused her to either curse and thrash or sob and sleep. Neutral emotions, that might appear on one's countenance as drifting, dreaming, or just going through the motions, were few and far between. Even when doing rote tasks like washing dishes or folding laundry she found herself slamming the soapy water with her fist or tossing a neatly folded towel into the air, already dense with her supercharged energy. Impulsive actions that splattered bubbles on her face and blouse or consumed her once-guarded work time with the task of having to scoop up crumpled laundry and fold, with more frustration, a second time.

A constant surge of memories and desires exploded from her mind like a missile aimed at her heart's growing chasm—burning her throat on the way down and igniting her voice with blue-hot fire, whether her words raged aloud or remained simmering beneath. She was becoming an animated collection of all the unspoken words and unresolved anger of her matriarchal ancestors. Every day, the blaze grew within her, waking another wounded ghost from her lineage of bold and beautiful, yet unfulfilled, women.

At the end of another tormented day, Mackenzie sat on her beach blanket, inches away from the shifting boundary where salt meets sand. Choosing to keep her eyes closed rather than gaze at another sunset without the man she loved sitting next to her, she could feel the hush of light leaving her makeup-free face and mostly exposed, sensitive skin.

Just beyond the vibration of her seething heart, a dark and jagged wall stretched along the sand, further than her line of vision. Formed by violent collisions, the scraping of glaciers, and the ocean's chiseling, earth's ancient carving served as a barrier between her and the sea, muffling the soothing sounds of the rolling surf. A pink haze swirled above her. Conditioned by occasional tourists who tossed crumbs, birds kept one eye on her, and the other eye on the water's surface, where dinner would more likely jump from.

She thought about how hunger forces eyes to stay alert and how her own appetite for life was diminishing. She wanted to fold herself into the enveloping beach scene, like hand-whipped cream, smooth, glossy, and sweet, and in danger of dissolving into an unappealing puddle for no obvious reason. She needed to look away or that which her eyes could see and her hands could touch would consume her. She did not want to be reminded of her ability to touch. Everything she could touch, that was not him, the one who ignited her desires—was destroying her. She could feel herself splintering from the inside.

The grains of sand surrounding her, once pleasing to run her hands across and push her feet into, now felt like a million tiny knives tearing into her. The pain reminded her that she was still alive, but she did not want to be reminded. She wanted to evaporate into the morning mist, no longer feeling the absence of his skin. She was in a state of suspended existence.

While sitting cross-legged on a handwoven blanket that she and her had ex-husband purchased when they traveled to Mexico one year before they decided to divorce, she looked toward the sun, a glistening gold jewel disappearing and reappearing beyond the pink clouds. The descending warmth was oozing down her body, like the hot chocolate frosting she poured over the top of her favorite cake, not made in nearly a decade. Her breath was slowing. With each exhale she felt her body settle into the sand, like cooled frosting puddling on a platter. Her fractured and stormy soul was collapsing inward toward her core.

She was just a few more deep breaths away from reaching her sacred center, but her mind, clinging to strands of doubt, was resistant. *Just breathe, she told herself. Just breathe. Release. Release. Release.*

Squeezing her eyes tighter did nothing to erase the image of kissing her lover goodbye; those thoughts were stuck on repeat. She wanted to fracture herself into a million pieces and scatter herself across the sand—let it absorb her. Let it transform her. Shaping broken pieces of her into polished sea glass that captured the rising rays, smoothing her sharp shards into an angelic display. Turning sorrow and all that cut her into glimmering pebbles, soft to the touch.

She wanted to be reduced to liquid, purified, then poured across the crest of an incoming wave, blending only slightly with the salty spray that created an imperfect arc, baptized by a glossy tint, withdrawing back to its origins, never to be seen again. If there was even the slightest chance that she could manifest wings, she would sacrifice her limbs then fly far away. The edge of the universe would not be far enough to escape the thoughts of him.

None of her desperate desires were possible. This truth she knew and loathed. This truth was an undisturbed side of the bed. It was tea for one. It was silence instead of shared laughter. This truth drowned her invincibility, delivering moments of panic that left her gulping for air before it resuscitated her with a heavy and hard-to-swallow acceptance.

Truth was a river that flowed steadily. Sometimes the flow was warm and calming and other times it shook her aggressively, aching her bones. The truth revealed its complexity with each passing day. From the truth she tried to run, but she could never look away.

Nine months had passed since she kissed Jason goodbye. His work as a photojournalist had called him overseas. He was reporting on the rebuilding of a region devastated by eleven years of war. He arrived in a location ravaged, but no longer under imminent threats. His assignment was only supposed to last six months, but in a profession that had hardened him, things were always subject to change. Text messages and FaceTime moments kept the pulse between the two of them steady, but it was not the same as a lover's touch, a morning whisper, or a midnight nudge.

Her mind could not erase the burning memory of his last kiss; however, her lips were losing the feel of his gentleness, a soft strength that had turned her bare skin and willing soul into a devoted lover who lingered in bed wrapped in the scent of him. She had planned on making him breakfast and a hot coffee to go before he left for his early morning flight, but their late-night lovemaking had caused her to sleep through his early morning tiptoeing.

She did not know, while she lay sleeping, that he had paused his rushing to gaze at her face, dreaming. His body warmed at the sight of her. His lingering revealed a man who did not want to leave her. Focusing on her eyes, closed, he took a picture of her with his cellphone before slipping it into the back pocket of his jeans. Not motivated by obsession but by absolute reverence and devotion—her sleeping frame was a priceless painting that he would carry with him.

Deep rest had erased tears from the night before. Her outward beauty was accentuated by an inner stillness that consumed him. A first for him. An award-winning photojournalist, the image taken of her the morning before he left her to travel would be his most cherished photo. One that he would share with no one, not even her. She was still dreaming in a room that was shifting from midnight cobalt to a creamy tangerine— his bitter cue that it was time to leave.

Their last night together had been a whirlwind of last-minute packing and passionate climaxing. The quickening of the clock kept pace with the union of their hearts, beating faster and faster as their bodies entwined around each other. Her hot breath became tiny embers on his earthy sweat. Two smoldering beings became one raging fire when fragmented flickers from the heavens fell on their bed that night. Never one to temper her pleasure, her moans, a blend of sultry screams and angelic songs, rushed through her apartment's cracked window, then whirled through the wind, before losing their fervor and descending to the sidewalk below where a dirty puddle absorbed the last of her sounds of ecstasy. Two tangled lovers falling into a deep sleep would have been the perfect ending to their moments wrapped in rapture, but reality ripped these lovers from each other. He needed to do some last-minute research before boarding the plane at 6 a.m.

She had imagined squeezing herself into his suitcase, when she was helping him fold and pack his lightly starched shirts. Like a delicate quiche, her body would flatten, and her heartbeat would slow to a barely traceable bleep. She would attempt these things for him and for him, she would save all her beats. She delighted at the thought of springing from his suitcase and into his arms after a long flight, but she knew the truth of her fantastical plight: even if she could have squeezed between the layers, she would not fit in. She was his favorite crumpled t-shirt, comfortably worn. At home, alone with her keyboard and her dreams, she would remain, while he flew to his important assignment, overseas.

The sleeping photo was not the only secret he kept from her. More than once during the days leading to his departure, he thought about inviting her to join him but to that offer, he never did commit. With his publisher, he could have pressed the issue of taking his writing girlfriend with him. He had paid his dues to a business that almost cost him his life, at least once, and his soul— well, he confessed to her that he had given that up long ago.

He no longer had anything to prove. Why not invite the distraction of her? She could fill her days with writing and his sleepless nights with her body and passion. She could have traveled with him at least part of the time. He chose to do none of these things. Not because he didn't love her. He loved her too much. She became his world, and he became hers, when they were together. Theirs, a love made for an alternative dimension, where love, not schedules, rules daily existence. A fiery love—they would burn each other up if they did not separate from time to time. A mutual knowing left unsaid.

So much had happened in their lives since he last kissed her. She brushed sand from her lips, as her mind began to drift back to the present, after losing sense of place and time during her morning meditation. She remembered how he traced her lips with the same finger he used to click his camera. Something he did when her mind spun itself into a cyclone, spinning and spilling wild thoughts across her tongue. She wondered if he would ever do that again. She wondered if his lips would feel the same or taste the same. She wondered many things.

Except for the other residents in her new quiet beach town and the stray dog that had appeared on her porch when she was moving in, she had spent the last nine months alone, three of those months getting situated in her newly acquired cottage by the sea. With her solitary existence, she was not troubled. She had made peace with the whispers and screams of loneliness long ago. They still lived inside her, but they no longer controlled her. They were not hers to control either. The different shades and shadows of loneliness did as they pleased. They were her messengers, her audience, and sometimes her judge and jury. Alone, her mind was its own universe that kept pushing beyond its container, protected by a woman who was no longer its god but its allowing creator.

She pulled her four-legged companion closer on the beach blanket. His panting, close to her left ear, comforted her. Sharing space with another living being was saving her. She wrapped her blanket around him. He did not need extra warmth during a summer morning, but she needed his. She needed to feel the source of his unconditional love next to her heart, less sure of love, or anything that truly mattered. The two of them, woman and canine, facing the rising sun. She leaned her head against his while he looked on. She cried at the beauty of it. She cried over the pain of the mere thought… what if she were here alone without the presence of this protective animal spirit?

She hadn't been looking and he hadn't been trying when she met the faraway man who consumed her. It had just happened—now a two-year love affair that began not by the eyes' attraction but by a heart's knowing. They had met at a yearly fundraiser that raised scholarship money for disadvantaged youth in the city. It was a longstanding and popular charitable event that attracted writers, scholars, great thinkers, and rich do-gooders willing to write big checks.

Wealthy attendees who were always looking for ways to transform the abundance of brains in the room into more profit for their portfolios: an unspoken agenda disguised as a "good cause" that hitched a ride along flowing hems and stitched itself into tailor-made trousers. They were the only two not chatting in the grand room. Clinking crystal glasses and exaggerated ideas flowing were a brilliant contrast to a room full of classic black. The two mingling misfits were drawn to each other. Perhaps to save themselves from the awkwardness of standing alone. Or perhaps their forward steps were preordained.

She felt her body exhale when he stood close to her. She told herself that it was just a relief to have someone to talk to, but she sensed something else going on. Her mind resisted this truth, but her tingly body knew. If anyone had noticed them talking that evening, they would have considered them to be long-term friends—or much more, with the ease at which their words and bodies interacted. Leaning toward each other, smiling, and laughing, their words and thoughts were free-flowing. Pausing periodically and intensely staring at each other, they had the look of in-sync soulmates, not two strangers who had just met.

After names were exchanged, "Jason," and "Mackenzie," he took the next step. With his eyes looking at the floor, he asked for her number. She found his shyness charming and refreshing. With their busy schedules it took two weeks for them to meet again. They met for coffee at a café halfway between her place and his. Back when she still drank it. She still lived in the city then, too. He came and went, as work dictated. An evolving companionship that was never predictable or overly scheduled. Every time they met, more of her old self fell away, allowing her to discover a passion within that she had known existed. A growing passion that slowly and effortlessly replaced everything that had been a distraction for her, before meeting Jason. The aimless busyness that had previously filled her free time, like shopping on a Saturday afternoon, buying things she did not need, or saying *yes* to cocktails with acquaintances who drank too much and who were always trying to fix her up, had been rewritten with thoughts of, or time with him. His dynamic presence in her life revealed greater depths to her woman's soul that was no longer satisfied by swimming in the shallow pool. Time fillers. Time killers. Meeting him revealed these truths. At first, she ignored these thoughts. She tried to stomp out a growing flame of awareness. She tried to outlaugh and outrun it, but eventually she stood still and let the fire of a fated love envelop her. She was made better for it. The flames burned away her skepticism and cynicism, clearing the way for delicate dreams to emerge. She should have been terrified, she should have felt exposed, but she had never felt more alive. With another person, she had never felt more at home.

Her heart and soul expanding with an awareness that she prayed would not forsake her, she had realized it was time to match her exterior surroundings with the internal joy and refinement that flowed through her. That awareness had made her smile. She needed to leave the noise of the city and find a place that nurtured her. She did worry that a longer drive to her might keep him away, but she decided she had to be true to herself, and if the two of them were meant to last, he would find his way.

His love and attention, which had stripped her of false living and woken her from the slumber of barely existing, might be the very thing that would drive them apart. Tasting love with depth had made her hungry for authenticity. She was now ready to thrive. Not just when they were together, but as an individual capable of sharing this grand discovery with the world. Love had revealed this much.

Armored with a greater sense of self and certainty, she made a bold decision two months after Jason flew to his assignment: she decided to sell her city apartment and buy a cozy cottage by the sea. She had imagined leaving New York City before. Never seriously though, until Jason stirred new life in her.

She had grown tired of the city noise and the constant chatter in her head, but she did have concerns. *Who would she be without the constant hum? Where would she go? Without city life to keep her occupied, who would she become?* In theory she could write anywhere, but could she? Hadn't the city flurry given her ideas and energy? It had, but maybe it was time for a change. She was unsure, but the not knowing excited her. *A change for her.* Love had given her courage. She knew what she needed to do.

As if being directed by a greater force beyond herself, she texted a realtor friend. Three hours later she had signed a listing agreement and two days later, on a Friday, her place was on the market. She had three offers on her apartment before the weekend ended. A bidding war ensued. Her place sold for ninety-three thousand dollars over asking. She was elated. She was terrified. *What had she done?* She wasn't yet sure, but she did decide there was no turning back.

Before the whirlwind of real estate activity, she had told Jason of her plans to sell her place during their Friday night call—a routine that did not always happen because his work situation was unpredictable. He was surprised by her news. He sounded somber when he told her he would miss making love to her above the sounds of the street and that he would never forget their last night together, there, in her place: a two-bedroom apartment in Chelsea purchased with her divorce settlement and a small inheritance. Her abode was packed with all she had collected during her ten years of living in the city and items she had brought with her from her previous home in Los Angeles, where she had lived with her husband for seventeen years. Theirs had been a drawn-out divorce. No children to bargain with, just plenty of assets to sort out. A college romance that should have remained that.

Letting go of a marriage that felt more like a roommate situation than a soul connection was like saying goodbye to a close friend who she might or might not see again. Now, letting go of cherished personal belongings twisted her emotions in ways that a divorce had not. The thought of clearing out closets, cupboards, and shelves made her want to coil into a fetal position to protect herself from the ripping away. It needed to be done, even though she wasn't ready. Deciding what to keep and what to toss was difficult at first, but something overtook her during the third day of the process—an overwhelming urge to be free. Of unnecessary things. Of her past. Of more to pack before moving again. She began to let go with wild abandon. Books. Clothes. Coats. Shoes. Old spices. Old makeup. Knick-knacks. Each box given to charity felt like a boulder lifted from her shoulders.

Two days before she was to close on her apartment, she drank a hot herbal tea on the bare floor in her mostly emptied-out living room. Rugs were rolled, boxes were stacked, and most of her furniture was covered. It was the first break she had taken in over a week, since beginning her frenzied clearing out. In that moment, with her body beginning to relax, she lifted her gaze from the floor to her recently cleaned windows. She noticed two mourning doves huddled close to each other on her balcony rail. She hoped their closeness was enough to protect their bird bodies from winter's chill. Their cooing duet unleashed in her a flow of tears. She cried for the rest of the day. She could not stop. When she fell asleep that night in her place for the last time, like her apartment, she had been emptied out.

CHAPTER 2

MACKENZIE HAD A GENERAL idea of what she was looking for when she began her seaside search but mostly, she was guided by a knowing that she would know the right place when she saw it. She felt homesick at the start of her quest; however, as she pressed on, she grew to love the freedom that accompanied letting go of her familiar walls. While searching, she stayed in hotels and Airbnb's and wrote at coffee shops or in her vehicle, a purchase made after selling her place. She had not needed an automobile in the city, but she and her used SUV, selected to keep her safe on wintry roads, became complementary traveling companions, venturing along the East Coast, looking for her next home.

As soon as she saw the beach bungalow, one week before spring, in the quiet seaside town of Green

Cliff, Maine, she was prepared to sign the contract. Her seaside discovery appeared perfect. The cottage was cozy. The cottage was secluded. The cottage was neglected. Birds had taken over the porch, and the façade was overdue a fresh coat of paint. Remnants of a garden remained. She noticed a few brown stem fragments pressed against the dry earth. Peas? Carrots? She wasn't sure.

Until that moment, she had not considered growing a garden. She had not considered growing anything. Now she imagined pushing her hands into the dirt. She imagined being surrounded by colorful marigolds and daffodils and flavorful vegetables. Excitement burst through her body at the thought of it. She wanted to shout from the cliff's edge at the possibility of it. The cottage was quiet perfection. It was a shabby heaven. It would soon be hers. This she was sure of. The cottage would give her just enough room for everything that she needed, which, other than her keyboard, a few books and clothes, a kitchen stocked with the basics, a bathroom with plenty of hot water, and his touch, wasn't much.

Something about this place woke in her an overwhelming urge to nurture and protect. Maternal stirrings that she had learned to suppress long ago. There had been moments in her younger years when she had longed for children. The longing did not derive from a need to have a child with her ex-husband—he did not want children. She had known and accepted this about him before they got married, but acquiescing to his choices did not squelch her own desires. While married, she often felt the yearning to experience pregnancy… to experience motherhood… to hold a child… her *own* child. These longings left a void in her soul and in her life. She attempted to cover up dreams of motherhood with more work. More work brought more income, and more income brought happiness into their marriage. A temporary happiness that never came close to softening the edge of her sadness, but she realized early in their marriage that there wasn't enough love to nurture two hearts let alone three, so she kept swallowing her maternal dreams along with her daily birth control pills. Both the pill and her emptiness had made her nauseous.

Those buried motherly desires erupted inside her when she stood on the front porch of the cozy place that she was desperate to own. She became a mixture of consuming fire and cleansing tears. She wanted to wrap her arms around the sullen frame and never let go. She wanted to chain herself to one of the peeling porch pillars to prove to every passerby, and every bird soaring above, that the roaming writer and the abandoned abode were meant for each other. A shabby cottage by the sea in desperate need of some tender loving care. So was she. A beautiful partnership they could be.

A tour of the cottage interior with a local realtor took less than ten minutes. Less than ten minutes to look in every cupboard, peer through four window blinds, scan two closets, look under two sinks, flush one toilet, and step into one shower. It was perfect.

Although she was prepared to toss her one suitcase inside and sign every document, the business of humans took precedence over affairs of the heart. A few restless days after falling in love with the cottage by the sea, she learned from her newly hired realtor that the cottage was involved in a lawsuit. Just one of several assets that heirs were fighting over since the previous cottage owner passed without a will. The five heirs were distant, at best, and it was doubtful any of them had ever stepped foot on the property that already felt like hers. She was disappointed though not defeated. She became fiercely determined.

Not willing to take chances with her dreams, she hired a real estate attorney experienced in contentious property situations. The attorney came with high praise and a high hourly fee. A moving expense that Mackenzie had not budgeted for but one she accepted as part of the battle to claim her plot of peace overlooking the sea. Both the silent cottage and the splashing waves were pulling her, even when she was far from their view. She prayed they would not pull her under.

She wanted to move in and get going with her new life, but life had other plans. Life always has other plans. Life can be cruel, stirring desires while simultaneously pausing or blocking their fruition. For several days after learning that the cottage would not be gained without a fight, she felt like a caged racehorse pacing in a tiny stall waiting for the metal door to lift. Becoming a wild mare, kicking, and grunting when the free, open field felt more like a cliff. In the stall she remained confined. She wanted to scream at fate. She wanted to find the five greedy heirs and plead her case. What she needed to do was calm down. She needed to carry on and take care of other responsibilities if she were to have a chance of taking care of the cottage: a dilapidated homestead that she longed to turn into a peaceful scene. A place where Jason could rest and be restored after his extended assignment. A place where he could let go of everything else and love her. This she was sure of.

From a dated and musty motel room, a few miles down the road from her dream, she regrouped. It took her a few days to handle a few pressing matters: extending the lease on her storage unit in Brooklyn (a less expensive option than those found in her old neighborhood); paying for a month's stay in the seaside motel; getting the oil changed in her car;

checking in with her newly hired attorney; listening to her publisher scold her for falling behind on her most recent deadline; and telling Jason about finding her dream home and the trouble and expense it was going to cost her.

"Congratulations!" he replied with a genuine tone that revealed his confidence in her. One word from him felt like a lifetime of understanding. No hesitation, just instant and authentic feedback. A childlike excitement like one might hear on Christmas morning when the "perfect" gift is unwrapped. Jason's hands were too far to touch her, but his words, one at a time, stitched themselves into a comforting blanket that wrapped around her.

"Thank you. I can't wait for you to see it!" she blurted back, then became instantly mad at herself for sounding like a schoolgirl. "Well, it's not mine yet, but it is going to be," she added. As soon as those words left her lips, doubt crept in. Holding that belief inside was like allowing a thousand soldiers to defend her cottage desires. Her defending army fled with her ecstatic words and made her vulnerable for self-doubt.

"Of course, it will be!" he assured her. "It is meant to be. You've been searching and searching, and this is the one; I can hear it in your voice. You sound more excited about this one than you ever did with the others."

He was right. It was the right cottage, and *he* was

the right one—two absolute truths. Words that she wanted to sling across the Atlantic toward him. Words that longed to clasp hands and dance with him. Words that wanted to arrange themselves into a sensual poem for him. Despite their persistent pushing, she would not let these words fly from her tentative lips. She would not let it happen again—saying too much to the man she could not touch. These thoughts, she needed to lock up. She clenched her teeth and squeezed every muscle to keep these truths from meeting the same fate as her inner soldiers, now scattered bits bonded to her escaped breath. Tiny defenders plucked from her soul, not capable of protecting anything—just casualties of her childlike optimism.

Cottage dreams and images of Jason on a bended knee appeared in her brain while he told her about interviewing a young father who had lost everything during the war—his wife, his baby girl, his home, his business, everything—and yet this young man found the strength to wake up every day, and to help rebuild his neighborhood and his livelihood, a jewelry and watch repair shop that had been in his family for three generations.

While trying to turn off her dreamy images of a future home and Jason's presence in it, and focus on his poignant storytelling, his steadfast professionalism and conviction, she asked him: "How does one lose everything and carry on?" A heartfelt question that acknowledged his interview mention and her engagement in the conversation, before her mind quickly drifted back to imagined images of him, sitting on her cottage porch… the two of them walking hand in hand across the sand… These stirring thoughts she could not turn off. She did not want to. The nearness of him, however far he might be physically, flipped switches in her body and her mind became a theater in the round when he appeared. Hearing the background noises of his environment made the experience more real than her ongoing daydreams. A thousand scenes of the two of them, swirling round and round and round.

"I suppose he hasn't lost hope," Jason replied, before a long pause silenced the conversation between her and him. Pauses highlighted his deep breathing and captured her attention even more than his words. She felt her body temperature and the oceanic tides within her begin to rise. She wanted to remain in this moment, hearing his breath like the night winds whipping through her during her evening walk, leaving no part of her, neither the corporal nor the spiritual, untouched. His rhythmic breath excited and soothed her. She closed her eyes and imagined him behind her. His skin on her skin. His hardness pressing against her lower back. His breath in her ear. He was near. She could imagine him. She wanted desperately to feel him.

"Mack, are you still there?"

"Oh, yes, I am sorry, yes, I am here, when do you think you'll get to come back to the States? For a visit, at least?"

"Did you hear what I said about the man I interviewed today? About him receiving a U.S. grant to purchase inventory for his business?"

"That is wonderful news," she responded, trying to hide her disappointment at having her own question left unanswered. She suddenly felt selfish for wanting Jason to drop everything and fly to her. He was doing good work, she reminded herself. He was sharing uplifting stories from an area in need of good news. He was sharing personal details about voices, both the buried and the living, that needed to be shared after being silenced by violence. With an attentive ear, a friendly demeanor, a camera, and a respected writer's pen, he was one of the many healers bringing resurrection to a region covered in ashes and unsettled ghosts.

She would not ask him again. "I am proud of you," she admitted with authenticity. She hoped he felt loved and validated.

"Thank you." His soft response eased her tense muscles. "I am not sure when we will finish… not sure when I will be able to fly home. My camera assistant was sick for a week, so that put us behind, and I am still trying to get an interview with the prime minister." His tone became noticeably agitated. "I want to come home, too. I am tired. I need a long hot shower and a comfortable bed."

The resignation in his voice made her ache to take care of him. "I need you," he confided. She could hear the longing in his voice, but what she could not see was his body sinking deeper into the only chair in his hotel room, a faded burnt orange with a few tears falling on the worn leather. Nor could she see him gazing at the last photo he took of her—the one that he looked at every night before he drifted off to sleep.

"I need you too," she confessed, her voice a fractured whisper fighting to disguise her profound loneliness. She needed to stay strong. She needed to stay focused on her own challenges: securing the title to her dream cottage. For the two of them, she dreamed.

"Keep me posted on the beach house. I know you'll get it!" She knew he was trying to leave her with something to smile about; he always did. "Get some writing done today."

She chuckled, "Goodnight. I will keep you posted about the cottage. Fingers crossed it all works out."

"It will and when it does, I will make love to you for a week on your private beach."

Her body hummed. "I can't wait. Talk soon."

"Bye. Talk soon."

Not soon enough she thought, as his voice

lingered in the room, long after the call ended.

She woke the next morning to what sounded like a chaotic blend of laughter and a warning siren. Impossible to tune out, the shrill, metallic sound consumed the quiet. Kids roughhousing in the hotel parking lot, she thought. Her mind may have been jolted awake, but her eyelids, heavy fortresses to the dream world that lay beyond, weren't ready to open to daylight. With her eyes closed she could see, hear, and touch Jason.

It felt like she was dropping into the pit of hell, as the piercing sound intensified outside her ground floor hotel room. *What the fuck?* Anger catapulted her from her hard bed, its own form of torture, toward the salt-stung window. She pushed aside the left panel of the burlap curtains which were made heavier by humidity. Through weathered glass and blurry vision, she watched the frenzied scene. Fighting over what looked like a discarded Happy Meal were the source of the screams. With beaks snapping and claws scraping against each other, two seagulls were going after each other like two mad drunks who had forgotten the reason for their first liquor-lit punch. The sight of the feathered pair lifting from the ground just long enough to peck at each other before darting away, only to return, made her laugh. The pitch of their fury made her shiver.

She was awake now, and with her sensual dreams of Jason interrupted, she was also irritated. She had not abandoned the constant noise of the city to be bothered by two deranged birds. Wearing only terry cloth shorts and a see-through bra, Mackenzie flung open the door and stomped her bare feet toward scattered burger and bun bits, picked up what she could then flung the parking lot food as far as she could. She felt a little better. She felt stupid. She prayed no one was snapping pictures of her from a hotel window. Her agent was already upset with her, though perhaps lunatic publicity might boost her next book release. The birds took flight, not to chase after the half-eaten prize but to get away from her, the wandering author who was doing her best to claw her way out of a life that no longer belonged to her and toward one that was aligned with her soul's calling.

Back in her hotel room, she brewed hot water for tea in her two-cup coffee pot then switched on the vintage television. Watching the news was a recent activity for her, beginning after Jason's departure. She was interested in only one kind of news story: one that might involve his reporting. No news about the recovering region her lover found himself in. The main story, airing across all local channels, was news about a Category Four hurricane twirling in the

Atlantic, threatening to touch down as a Category Five along the shores of Boston before forging further north. She considered how ill-prepared she was for a fierce storm; then she scribbled a note on her writing pad: Stock Up!

Her thoughts quickly turned to *her* empty cottage. *Would the abandoned structure survive a severe storm?* Maybe she could use potential destruction of the cottage as leverage with the greedy heirs. No, she quickly told herself, even if the storm made it that far north, that gave her only two days to play that hand. It took her that long just to get through to her attorney, let alone have the documents drafted that could spell out the impending doom.

The spinning storm system early in the hurricane season was over four hundred miles away. One was brewing much closer: stress, worry, and uncertainty had hijacked her sleep-deprived brain. Stopping her runaway thoughts was like asking the ocean to stop ebbing and flowing. Directing her anxiety toward the depths, she threw on a sweatshirt, laced up her sneakers, grabbed her beach blanket, then headed to the shore. She spent the next hour falling into a deep meditation. The gentle waves in front of her began to calm the cyclone forming inside her.

When she opened her eyes, she noticed what looked like a ship made of cement in the distance and she sensed goosebumps on her legs when the ascending sun vanished behind a dark gray ink blot. She did not want to leave this captivating seaside painting, but she needed to get on with her day: prepping for a possible storm, calling her lawyer, and adding *at least* five thousand words to her manuscript before nightfall, or she would suffer a scolding from her publisher. Survival, dreams, and the demands of others motivated her to stand, brush off the sand, and get a move on. Once on her feet, she traced her fingers down her legs toward the ground, then up to the heavens before shaking off her blanket and walking to her hotel shower—a shower that sounded like demons were escaping from hell when she turned the rusty dial to hot.

Mackenzie spent the next two weeks buried in her manuscript, a sequel to her last book what would be her fourth novel, if she made it to the finish line. Other than one call to her lawyer a few days prior, she had not talked to anyone in thirteen days, including Jason who was working in a remote location. They had spoken two Fridays prior. He told her he was going to be swamped with what he hoped would be final interviews and the needed collection of area footage. Her elation hung on his "final" words. Words she had to remind herself of, again and again, when the longing for him became too much.

Her last conversation with another human in the flesh had taken place between her and the cashier at a market a few miles down the road. Hurricane Bertha had been an invitation to everyone nearby to visit the small shop and stock up on supplies. As an outsider in the seemingly tight-knit, tiny community, she felt uncomfortable grabbing the last bag of potatoes or an extra roll of toilet paper, but the imminent demands of survival can turn even the most carefree into a focused prepper. She collected enough items to sustain her for at least a week then returned to her writer's den, taking the long route by way of her hopeful residence. She stopped her car in front of the abandoned cottage that seemed to call to her for rescue. She sat for a few minutes before deciding that walking around the property would be too painful; she needed to reserve her emotional stamina for more writing.

The cottage was beginning to look more like a ghost than a livable abode. One that might disappear if her hands attempted to feel its peeling surface. She heard her editor's voice rattle in her mind telling her to get a move on… stop dreaming about what might be and turn your attention toward what you're contractually obligated to deliver, the voice demanded. She was desperately trying to focus on the faraway voice punctuated with the urgency of the city, but it was being muted by soothing waves. She understood and accepted what she had previously and willingly committed to—writing a fourth book—but she was not ready to drive away from the cottage scene in front of her. *Not yet.* She started the vehicle's ignition so that she could roll down the windows. Her frustration over the situation was elevating the temperature in her four-wheeled observatory.

A wind carrying traces of ancient Viking strength and dragon fire whipped through the vehicle's open windows, lifting her long tangled locks, and scattering loose papers that had been neatly stacked in the back seat. There was a time when such an occurrence of disorder would have sent Mackenzie into a cursing frenzy. She had discarded those quick-tempered reactions along with the clothes and a life she had outgrown. She closed her eyes and let the Atlantic's gust penetrate her hidden fortress, guarded by flesh, muscles, bones, and rivers of blood.

Five minutes or five hours, she wasn't sure how much time had passed when she opened her eyes again. With her hair covering and sticking to her face she was not able to see the cottage porch that called for her during her restless dreams. She let her thoughts flow, and she let her eyes remain hidden.

With the humidity, her hair never dried thoroughly. She had given up on trying to style it. She was learning to let go of the stylish and structured life she once knew, the one she had clung to—the overcommitted life that had replaced marriage and children. A former life where every daily moment was planned, and every hair was neatly in place. She began to laugh at the fear she had felt about letting it all go: her apartment, her cleaning lady, her impressive calendar and pressed clothes, her hair stylist and manicurist, and all the other service professionals who helped her fit the role of a successful (enough) writer living a coveted life on New York's west side. They were all sad to see her go, for a minute, until her time slot was quickly filled.

Her laughter heightened to hysterics when she brushed back her hair and caught a glimpse of herself in the car's rearview mirror. If her hair grew another inch, she would need to trade in her sturdy SUV for a sporty convertible. Hysterical laughter became the soundtrack for her tumbling tears. A soul's cleansing absorbed by the bottom lining of her terry shorts and decorating her bare legs with salty drops. A rough and raw blend of laughter, tears, and wild and loose curls, she had never felt so beautiful; she had never felt so free. The last tear and the last chuckle were the opening act for the main show: a woman transformed. A woman lighter in spirit and deeper in thought, now ready to embrace her untamed look as part of her new life… a seaside writer and a returned man, by her side.

CHAPTER 3

"ANOTHER SIXTY THOUSAND," her lawyer told her.

"What the hell! My offer is already fifty thousand over list price."

"Give me some time to think about it," she fumed into the mouthpiece of the hotel's rotary dial phone. The one with the short cord that tethered her to the cup-stained desk. If the cord was any longer, she might use it to hang herself.

"Ok, I will stall them, but hurry, they have three other solid offers."

"Fuck, ok."

She already knew the answer, but she had to hold on to *some* dignity, at least the appearance of some anyway. The greedy bastards were kidnappers, holding her heart and her seaside dreams for ransom.

She grabbed her purse which she had reduced from a stuffed one full of urban necessities to a small over-the-shoulder sling bag, just big enough for her ID, credit card, phone, glasses, lip gloss, tissues, and hotel key. Already dressed from her morning produce shopping, she slammed through the door, loud enough to disturb her hotel neighbors but not loud enough to be heard by the keepers of her dreams: the four heirs pulling her purse strings and mocking her fragile heart. For the four of them she let out a scream in the parking lot on her way toward the cottage.

Five heirs had become four when it was determined through DNA testing that one claimant held no biological connection to the previous owner of the cottage. Testing their saliva for a biological match was a necessary step in the legal entanglements she found herself in. One less greedy hand did not equate to lesser demands; the four remaining salivating dogs were more than eager to grab the fifth's vacated share. Blood drawn not spilled, though it did feel like a violent war, in her own soul. One more trial in the annoying and expensive court proceedings that had dragged on for two months before bringing her and the four heirs to what would hopefully be the final battle, ending with her standing victoriously on the hill next to her dream cottage. So close to signing on the bottom line, she was. So close to having her belongings in storage shipped to her new home, the one that would become her child and her keeper. She was so close to welcoming Jason home. The last conversation with him had revealed he felt the same, but there were many obstacles yet to overcome before he arrived in her new home.

The heirs were greedy parasites, dangling a carrot in front of her. They had not done a damn thing to earn that cottage, and she doubted they had had any involvement with the old man who had once planted vegetable seeds in its now dried-up garden.

Their cash demands made her own blood boil and trying to make the right decision for her future split her brain in two. She needed to see the cottage one more time before agreeing to empty out her savings account. The practical and prudent side of her personality motivated her to visit the cottage, hoping to find something wrong with the place. *Anything.* She needed to walk from the hotel to the abode, like a neglected child caught up in a contentious custody battle, with only one parent offering unconditional love. Mackenzie needed to see the place, and she also needed to release the steam that was brewing inside her. Each step along the dirt road fueled her frustration, turning her churning core into an underwater volcano. Her escalating anger was a greater threat to the town's residents than the storm that had lost its punch before it had a chance to stir the waters near the town's shore. A warning should sound, for all approaching to run and take cover. A building resentment in her, yes, but she was no real threat. She would stand and let herself be consumed by her own lament before harming anyone in the sleepy town that was already feeling like home.

She took the final few steps to the top of the hill, where the cozy cottage waited. Now eye level with the aged windows, she knew—she had no doubt—for that cottage, she would bleed out.

With fire shooting from her fingertips, she pressed her finger on the most recent number in her cell phone... the number that made her blood thicker and her wallet thinner. "Tell them they have a deal," she said, "I will wire the funds by the end of the day." The child in her danced.

Two weeks had passed since she was handed the key to her new home, on the porch that creaked a "welcome" when they stood near the door. One rusty and slightly bent key was all she was given. The right key was enough. She unlocked the door that led to the home's interior and to her inner peace, not an instant and full immersion of mind, body, and spirit, but she was finally stepping in.

After a quick inspection of the property and a brief conversation with her realtor, she was left alone in the empty home. *Her home.* A phrase that tumbled, unbelievably, through her mind, now freed and floating in a state of seaside euphoria and disbelief. A dream of living in a quiet cottage by the sea had come to her when she was still living in Los Angeles, embroiled in a stormy divorce. She had pushed that quiet dream aside, telling herself she was just needing an escape, that small town living was not for her. She told herself that the familiar noise and pace of a large city was a better fit, so off to New York she went after the final papers were signed and recorded. Familiar yet far enough away. Over time she had learned that no matter how far one runs, dreams remain. She paused for a moment, standing in the middle of a dream she could now see, breathe, hear, and touch.

She opened the front door, with all the vigor that a new life stirs, then she pried open the four windows, stuck together with the corrosion of neglect. She sat crossed-legged on the bare floor, rested her arms on her legs, then closed her eyes. The cross-breeze carrying the scents of late spring calmed her body. Her mind followed and responded with a release of emotion that rivaled the crashing waves, two hundred feet from her open front door. Like the turbulent seas coughing up brokenness from its depths, and splintered wood from its surface, her mind began to purge.

A surge of tears became an emotional tsunami over the wall she had built over the last few months. A wall, built to protect her dreams from everything that could go wrong, had been formed from curses, prayers, and pleas, cemented together with her tears. Working tirelessly to keep the wall fortified, she had barely slept. She had been one woman pushing against the wall. She had been a thousand women, all at once, patching fractures in the wall. Never leaning for too long but running like hell from one breach to the next. At times her womanly strength shrunk to a shadowy sliver, barely existing along the imagined wall.

With her eyes closed and her body resting on the bare cottage floor, during what would be her first night in the cottage, she saw herself smashing the protective wall with a sledgehammer. With the mighty muscles of a fierce warrioress, she smacked the wall once, twice… a thousand times, until it was reduced to rubble and bone-colored dust, rising. The woman in her mind's eye dropped the sledgehammer on the smoldering pile. She felt her body relax and her face warm after the symbolic cloud she stood under tore suddenly and violently.

Then, in her daydream, she saw Jason in the distance under the golden sun's full rays. The entire scene was a conjuring of her mind, but she knew it would not be long before they were in each other's arms. It would not be long before he kissed her salty neck, a sensual thought that rippled through her, causing her to bolt from the floor.

She twirled. She danced. She cried. She screamed. She collapsed. With her sweatshirt as a pillow, she fell into a seven-hour dream.

Her eyes, the first part of her body to wake, noticed an outstretched right arm. It must be hers she rationalized, but it felt like it belonged to someone else. She was certain the old wood floor had transformed itself into a living tree, winding its roots around her while she slept because she could not seem to lift her body from its grip. Too weak to pull herself up, she rolled over on her back.

Her eyes now looking up, she noticed a sizeable crack along the ceiling. She heard a cash register ding. She closed her eyes and told the annoying bean counter in her brain to shut the fuck up. "We'll get to it," she said out loud. "Just let me enjoy the fact that I made it here!" "Here" was in a rundown cottage by the sea. For the first time in a long time there was nowhere else she wished to be.

It would take the movers eight days to deliver her belongings from her Brooklyn storage unit. "Busy season," they told her. With only a suitcase and a laptop when she first stepped into the cottage, she was not prepared for house-living, so other than the first night in her new home, which had nearly destroyed her body, she kept sleeping at the hotel, rushing off early every morning to spend her days at the cottage. Connected to her phone's hotspot, she typed on the bare floor, taking frequent walk breaks to the shore. She was putting the final touches on her fourth novel's first draft before sending the 93,742-word document to her editor. Despite the constant presence of her publisher's demands, her days had a peaceful rhythm—an easy pace she had never experienced in the city. She felt content. She heard quiet. She saw beauty. Her soul was home.

Moving day had brought her belongings and a surprise to her front porch when the movers were carrying in her plastic-wrapped couch.

"Is he yours?" she asked.

"No, looks like you bought a house and a dog," the oldest-looking of the three movers told her with a smile that revealed more gum than teeth.

"Looks like I did," she smiled back, squinting when the day's brightness flooded her eyes. "Come here boy," she called to the dog.

The dog did not come, but he did not run either. She went inside, filled with water a Styrofoam container that had held her lunch ten minutes prior. She placed the container under the dog's nose, then petted him across the top of his head. With her right pointer finger, she traced a thin line of white that sliced through his crown's black. Her touch seemed to relax his sand-covered body. She knelt near the container and met the dog at eye level. She became very emotional when she looked into his eyes. Deep dark dog eyes revealed a sadness she knew all too well. Words were not needed at the soul level. With that first look, trust was formed. She had a sense that she and the stray dog would get along just fine.

She tossed a stick to him from her front porch, in between sips from her morning tea. She gave up trying to read emails from her laptop and watched the dog instead. His black coat now shone after a proper cleanse given under the leaky garden hose and his hesitant movements that first greeted her had been replaced with energetic leaps onto the front porch when he returned the tossed piece of driftwood.

A visit to the town vet had taken care of his shots and revealed he was a three-year-old Border collie who did not have a chip. The news of his free-dog status gave her permission to fall even more in love with him. He was hers and it would not require a fight. She named him Conan, the middle name of one of her favorite authors. With his curious and intelligent nature, the name suited him. She had him chipped should his curious nature cause him to wander away from her.

A few days of proper dog food and hearty hugs from her had transformed the stray into an alert companion. Taking care of him was changing her, too. He was becoming an endearing presence in her life, with his early morning puppy kisses from the side of the bed, his pouncing on every piece of crumpled packing paper, his tilted head when she read book passages to him, and his deep barks when the mailman delivered mail to the rusty mailbox at the end of her drive. She had dreamed about a seaside home long before she began looking for one and now, two weeks into her new residence, the unexpected four-legged wanderer was helping her breathe life into this home. Her entire body smiled at the thought of the new life and surroundings she found herself in, a warm feeling that softened her intense longing for Jason. She contemplated how a little bit of love and attention can transform another living being. She hoped this would be true for the love of her life. She couldn't wait for her faraway man to meet her four-legged friend. She was confident that Conan had enough love in his canine heart for both her and Jason.

So, there she was, two weeks officially owning the home that her heart had been searching for long before the actual search began, six days of unpacking, organizing, and scheduling subcontractors for the needed repairs before Jason arrived. She had a long list of things to take care of before his August flight. After a few phone calls and working out the details, she and Jason decided that he would fly directly to Maine, then, when the time was right, they would make the drive back to the city to gather a few of his things from his apartment. After a lot of thought and discussion it was decided that he would keep his city apartment. He was sure they would enjoy it again, someday. The details of their future held questions and uncertainty. She also believed their future held love.

She was relieved to have Conan back home with her, where he belonged. Final floor repairs had forced her to kennel him with the vet for four days. She was not sure if he wanted to play with or attack the wood-sanding machine, so she thought it best to separate him from the stressful situation. It broke her heart to leave him, but she needed to protect him.

Evenings had been empty and quiet without him. No panting, no sweet stares, no leg rubs, or nail clicks on the hardwood floor. Just the sound of waves and occasional seagull squawks.

After three months in her new place, her ears were beginning to distinguish wave sounds. Some days the waves sounded like they might crash into her front door and other days, like today, they sounded like a lullaby, calming her nervous energy. She only had a few minutes before she needed to drive to the airport to pick Jason up. *Finally.* Nine months of FaceTime calls, desperate longings for his hands on her body and his deep whispers in her ear, a pillow that had absorbed her tears, overwhelming sadness over his absence, worry about his welfare, and then the call that tore through those moments, like a thousand bullets piercing her from every direction.

She stopped herself from thinking too long about that late night life-changing interruption: the phone call that ripped her from her planned future and peaceful dream. She needed to get going. Having never been to Houlton International Airport, she was not exactly sure where she was going, and she did not want to be late. She did not want Jason waiting at the airport without her. She needed to keep it together. She needed to stay strong. For him. She went to the bathroom, flushed her new toilet, looked at herself in the lowered mirror one last time before scanning the interior of her cottage.

She hoped the changes made over the last twelve weeks would accommodate his needs.

Her place had been a flurry of activity; sweaty men who cursed on occasion and the constant presence of flying dust had forced her and Conan to spend a few nights in the same hotel she thought she had escaped from. Knowing their hotel stay would be temporary eased her mind. Fortunately, the hotel was pet friendly and Conan had been a well-behaved guest. She would have slept in her car if need be. She would have gone without sleep for one hundred weeks if it meant making her lover's homecoming as perfect as it could be. Nothing was completely perfect. This much she knew. Not with her place and certainly not with life, but the changes made to her place were accommodating, and their love was all-encompassing, which felt like enough. The three of them together would be more than enough. She grabbed her purse and Conan's things before the two of them made their way down the newly installed front porch ramp before getting into her car. With her furry sidekick in the back seat and she in the driver's seat, she started her car. She took a deep breath then put the car in drive before making her way down the newly smoothed gravel in front of her cottage, turning toward the quiet street.

Traffic down the road that led to her place was mostly nonexistent. Pausing to look both ways was an act of prudence more than a necessity but doing so gave her a chance to look at her freshly painted cottage in the car's rearview mirror. The neglected abode had been transformed into a beaming home. She smiled. She saw Conan in the mirror. He was smiling too. The cozy place and Conan's love felt like the family she had spent a lifetime longing for. The man she had fallen deeply in love with sitting next to her would complete this family portrait. She drove away from the cottage starting the over two-hour drive to the airport, where the love of her life would be landing. She spent the long drive breathing strength into all the nervous and unsure parts of herself while filling Conan's ears with all the beautiful things she loved about Jason. She hoped her storytelling would make him less of a stranger when canine and man officially met at the airport.

She was not sure about the rules of taking dogs into the airport, but she had seen enough pets when she travelled so she assumed it would be fine. After all, they weren't boarding, they were just picking up. They were a few minutes early and Jason's flight was a few minutes late. She was relieved. She needed a few minutes to calm down and just breathe. She found an out-of-the-way spot for her and Conan to wait. She had brought dog treats, but so far, she had not needed to reach for them. He sat next to her right leg watching people and a few other pets hustle by, never getting upset by any of it. Conan's calm nature was comforting to her. She had been hopeful he would show qualities of being a solid service dog and he was living up to her expectations.

She felt weeks' worth of tension leave her body in one expansive exhale. There was nothing to do now except breathe and wait. She tried to imagine what Jason might look like and how she would respond to his physical changes. She wondered what he was thinking. She wondered what the flight home had been like for him. Her mind was imploding from all the thinking. She knelt with Conan, pulled him close to her, then closed her eyes. She stayed in that position, with her and Conan's heads close to each other, until she received a text from the man who caused electricity to pulse through her veins.

I've landed. Just a few more minutes. Will be first one off. I have an escort.

I am here, she typed back.

She fought back the tears, then lifted herself from the ground before walking a leashed Conan as far as the two of them could go without breaching security. Like a curtain being drawn back, a group of about eight people dispersed, revealing Jason. She could no longer hold back the tears. They poured out of her. Never one to cry in public, she no longer cared. She was not the woman she once was, in many ways. She was not crying because he was being wheeled to her in a wheelchair, she was crying because he was there, because she would finally get to kiss him and feel his hands on her skin. He saw her and he began crying, too. It took every ounce of discipline within her body to not sprint past the security guards dressed in black and blue and fall at Jason's knees. Those last few inches to her felt like miles and the last few seconds felt like a century.

At last, they were next to each other. She no longer had to look up to stare into his eyes, but she could finally meet his eyes, and they revealed what she loved most about him—the depths of him. She let herself forget about everyone around her and she fell into his arms. Bent over him, she rested her head on his right shoulder. Her lips were close to his left ear. Their solo sobs blended into one undulating emotional wave that lasted several minutes before they were finally able to speak to each other.

She stood up, then rummaged through her purse for tissues. She found them then handed one to Jason before taking one for herself. Their crying turned to laughter as their reunion revealed a love like neither of them had ever experienced.

"This is Conan," she told him, gesturing with her hand toward Conan.

Jason extended both his hands to Conan who, without hesitation, met them.

"Hi Conan, I've heard so much about you. I have

a feeling you and I are going to become the best of friends."

Mackenzie stepped back and let the two of them have space to get acquainted. She wondered if Conan recognized Jason's voice from their many FaceTime calls. Their airport greeting would just be a formality. A beautiful one, she hoped.

The three of them made their way to the baggage claim area, with the assistance of the airport attendee who agreed to help them to her car. It would take some time and practice figuring out how to make their way through life now that Jason was wheelchair-bound. With the assistance of time, at least one more surgery, and ongoing physical therapy his disability's permanent or temporary status would be revealed.

Mackenzie tipped the attendee who courteously placed one large suitcase and a smaller bag, containing a laptop and camera equipment, in the back of her SUV while she situated Conan in the back seat. She had stocked her fridge, cleaned every counter and corner, and did laundry the day before and with her manuscript with her editor, the only thing left to do was drive to their quiet little house by the sea and love and comfort Jason.

Six months had passed since she had first wheeled Jason up the ramp that led to her—now their—new home. Conan was by his side as she leaned her body into the wheelchair that held his six-foot frame, lighter in weight and with less leg muscle than when he had left, what felt like a lifetime prior.

From that day on, Conan never left Jason's side. During his doctor and physical therapist appointments and grocery visits and all the other boring tasks that can fill up a day, Conan was there, observing and attentively loving, as only "man's best friend" can. She knew Conan was special when she first met him, but she had no idea just how important he would be in their lives and for that reason she sometimes called him her little angel.

She was inside working on her fifth novel while dog and man enjoyed their morning routine on the front porch. With his strong arms not noticeably affected by the accident, Jason was able to toss the piece of driftwood much further than she could. She loved watching the two of them—so much that she sometimes had to close the living room curtain to get any work done. Not today though. Today she let their joyful and playful presence take precedence over her word count. Their toss and fetch routine not only kept Jason's arms active, the tossing also allowed him to forget about his injury.

A serious back injury that his New York doctors believed—through Jason's perseverance and the advances of rehabilitative medicine and targeted therapy—had a chance of becoming part of his history, not a detriment to his future mobility. Familiar with covering wars, he was now fighting his own, every therapy session and careful movement, a quiet battle he approached with the same determination he had brought to the farthest corners of the earth.

She had a long ramp constructed that led to the beach, allowing Jason to visit the waves at his leisure. With Conan as his constant companion, it was a place where Jason spent many hours contemplating his life—a quiet stretch of shoreline where the rhythm of the tide seemed to steady what had once been unmoored. It was here he had begun typing his memoir: reflections on his years as an international photojournalist, chasing light and truth through places that had mostly long since turned away from him.

His career had ended abruptly on a narrow road cutting through a landscape still bearing the scars of war: buildings hollowed, earth unsettled, silence too heavy to be mistaken for peace. It was meant to be his final assignment, a last collection of images from a remote and forgotten place before returning home to Mackenzie. The jeep he had been traveling in lost control without warning, the sudden violence of it at odds with the stillness surrounding them. Metal twisted. Glass scattered like fragments of a story cut short. In the aftermath, he was left on the side of the road—alone beneath an open sky, breath shallow, body broken—with a fractured pelvis and severe damage to his lower lumbar region. He had spent years documenting destruction from a distance, lens between himself and the world. But in that moment, there was no distance left—only the stark realization that the life he had been racing toward, and the one waiting for him at home, had shifted irrevocably before he could reach it.

That same ramp later led the three of them, along with a local minister and a kind neighbor, to the water's edge on a night that felt suspended in time. A full moon stretched itself across the surface of the sea, its light dancing in quiet ripples that shimmered at their feet. The air was thick with the tang of salt, and a gentle breeze stirred the hems of Mackenzie's dress and Jason's jacket, brushing against their skin as if the night itself was participating in the ceremony. The tide whispered in steady rhythm, a soft accompaniment to the hushed voices around them, while Conan sat faithfully nearby, ears perked, his gaze moving between them, grounding the magic in something tenderly familiar.

Bathed in that silvery glow, they faced one another—no grand audience, no spectacle—only the quiet presence of those who had walked beside them, and the life they had nearly lost. Their hands trembled slightly as they clasped them, fingers intertwining with a mix of excitement and reverence; a single tear glimmered on Mackenzie's cheek, catching the moonlight like a tiny star. The moonlight softened every edge, casting them in a gentle radiance as they spoke their vows, voices steady but full, the words *I do* carrying more truth than either had ever known.

It was not just a union, but a return—something reclaimed at the water's edge, where truth had risen before them and love, at last, was no longer waiting. Here, in the cool hush of night, with waves curling around their ankles and Conan resting nearby, the world felt still and sacred, bearing witness to the quiet miracle of a life remade.

Although she had made a career out of writing creatively, Mackenzie could never have imagined this life—one shaped not by plans but by the quiet persistence of love. A life shared with a man who had walked through darkness and returned, carrying both scars and wisdom, and a devoted stray who had claimed them as his own. The days were far from perfect, filled with small challenges and the occasional ache of the past, yet each evening held a richness she had once only written about: the golden hush of sunset on the beach, the whisper of waves along the ramp, the soft presence of a hand she could finally trust to hold her own. It was a life built slowly, fiercely, and entirely real—a life full of love. Finally.

HER COTTAGE BY THE SEA
(MAY 2021)

Curtains swaying
a soft lift and gentle dip
a peaceful rhythm
matching the rise and fall
of their replenishing breath

Hues changing
a floating canvas
a fleeting Pissarro
filtering the pink sunrise
transforming walls inside

Senses stirring
a dream scene blurring
a mind's eye releasing
ushering in discoveries
in joy and carefree play

Fingers typing
a mind sparking
a coffee pot brewing
eyes still closed she
feels her lover's gaze

Skin warming

a passion igniting
a low tide revealing
what was once hidden
now brilliant and bare

Here, suspended
between sleep and awake
she will linger
just a few more minutes
inhaling the possibilities
bathing in the infinite

soaking in the ocean breeze
basking in her lover's radiance

Her eyes opening, her body drifting in a dream
soothing curves set against the cresting sea
they find each other and stare into the deep

Waking to a new day with endless possibilities,
where wild and untamable rise and merge
with soft and sensual in her cottage by the sea

HER COTTAGE BY THE SEA
(AUGUST 2021)

Slowly, she traced the smooth edge
of the top curve of her steamy cup. Smooth, it was,
under a fingertip that had felt his lips, soft to her
touch.
Knees tucked under her chin, wrapped in a soft
blanket
with hanging fringes swaying in the gentle wind.
Her body warmed by thoughts of him.
A smile birthed in her center, then flutter it did,
away from her edges, toward him—
the one tossing driftwood toward a stray
that had found the two of them.

A finger tracing, a mind remembering
their night before, that held radiant stars,
both near and far. Internal beats
did rise and blend with the changing hues
that began fireside then singed the crisp page
of a golden day. A passion that did pulse and vibrate
beyond their bare and salty skin—reaching other
worlds,
it did extend.

Her tracing meditation paused when she felt his
stare.

On her love, with chest bare, her eyes did gaze,
and on him her eyes remained. The solo butterfly
that fluttered from her core, now thousands
fluttering around him and the rolling shore,
where he stood tall, like Chrysos,
bathing in golden splendor,
flooding her in rapture.

HER COTTAGE BY THE SEA
(DECEMBER 2021)

A morning spent tracing curves
with slow and deliberate fingertips.
They release a power that contradicts—
soft, sensual, and delicate
yet, they spark a fire within.
They form the shape of words
absorbed by her salty and sandy skin.
Unspoken words turn to ash when they are drawn in
to a body that pulses with the cosmos
when he ignites the universe and splinters time,
like the god of thunder and sky.

Watching the sun rise over the ocean,
the two entwined glow in silence
in a cottage now painted golden.

He sees the glistening sea
in her eyes
and in his
she sees the depths

ABOUT THE AUTHOR

A WRITER OF POETRY and poetic prose, Michele Lee Sefton is a veteran English teacher who left the classroom in 2019 to develop her writing voice. She has since been published in various anthologies and platforms, including *Piper Poetry Month Anthology* through the Virginia G. Piper Center for Creative Writing at Arizona State University.

Collaborating with her artist daughter during the pandemic, she published a series of illustrated poetry chapbooks: *Being a Woman: Overcoming*, *Being a Woman: Becoming*, and *Being a Woman: Forthcoming*. In 2020, she published a collection of poems to celebrate the one-year anniversary of her blog, *My Inspired Life: A Poetic Journey*. Her titles *Her Coastal Cottage: Where Truth & Love Rise and Honeysuckle Heat* offer readers the author's vivid poetic prose in novella length.

Jade's Broken Bridge (2025) is her debut novel. She continues to publish creative projects under her imprint, Tumbleweed Spirit Press. Michele Lee enjoys sharing and connecting on her writing and photography blog, dancing with other expressive women, and working with Sandra Marinella, the author of *The Story You Need to Tell*, co-facilitating narrative therapy workshops.

* 9 7 9 8 9 9 9 1 5 0 6 2 2 *